AF138811

Dedicated to my Mother

Ursula Hess

Bluemoon stroll with Paul

A collection of ten stories
from Alice's Universe.

Translated from German
by Olga Shimell

Bibliografische Informationder Deutschen Nationalbibliothek:
Die Deutsche Nationalbibliothek verzeichnet diese Publikation
in der Deutschen Nationalbibliografie; detaillierte bibliografische
Daten sind im Internet über www.dnb.de abrufbar.

Herstellung und Verlag:
BoD – Books on Demand, Norderstedt

ISBN: 978-3-7392-1488-7

Index

Blue

Blue is my favourite colour. Not that I chose it myself; no, that's not how it happened. It came about almost by accident, one evening during one of our regular showdowns in the bathroom. As usual, we were arguing about which toothbrush belonged to whom and I was getting on everyone's nerves whining about wanting my flannel. It was by no means clear which one was mine and that led to yet more noisy arguments. The whole situation seemed impossibly tricky to us, but on that fateful evening our mother decided to intervene and sort the matter out once and for all. She entered the foaming scene with an air of determination and placed three cups on the shelf by the washbasin – one red, one green and one blue.

«One each», was her only comment.

Puzzled, we first looked at her and then at each other. My brother was first to react. He quickly chose the green cup with an air of self-confidence and beamed like a victorious king. My sister then grabbed the red one, which meant it was my turn to beam with joy, since it was the cornflower blue one that I'd liked best from the start. Our new system worked beautifully. From now on I was the one with the blue toothbrush, blue flannel, blue pencil case or the blue bike. From that evening onwards the colour blue had become, as I pointed out at every opportunity, an intrinsic part of me. I even wrote it in all the friendship books. Back then we called them poetry albums and filled them with supposedly the most important bits of information about ourselves and our favourite things and pastimes. The first question that came after name, nickname and date of birth was about one's favourite music. My answer tended to be either «The Beatles» or «Stevie Wonder», but more often than not Stevie Wonder won that spot. When it came to my favourite book, I cheated because «The Red Silk Scarf» didn't quite fit into my blue world. I therefore put one of De Cesco's other works, «The Turquois Bird» instead, and that fitted beautifully. Because of this book I was also certain that I would one day marry an Indian, just like it happened in «The Turquois Bird». Well, that part of my life turned out quite differently, but that's another story. The list of favourites continued and after the book came the favourite flower, which in my case was the delphinium. And then there was the favourite hobby, of course. I was always tempted to put «dreaming» but since my sister insisted that it was more like my permanent state rather than just a hobby, I usually settled for «reading». The last part was supposed to contain a few meaningful words which were to provide a lasting memory of me - or of whoever wrote an entry into the book. Here you found all kinds of rhymes and verses like «Talk is silver, silence is golden» or «Roses are red, violets are blue, I have a friend and that friend is you» and so on. And somewhere among all this there was of course the question about your favourite colour. Blue. Blue was my thing.

I even devoted years of my life to collecting blue words. I could easily have put that down as my hobby. Bluebell, blueprint, blueblood, I couldn't get enough of these words. I used them all the time, even if they didn't make any sense in the context. Often I had no idea what they actually meant, like «blue moon stroll» for example. That sounded strange and mysterious and I imagined that it was something reserved for just a select few and of course I counted myself in that number. Whenever I was cross with my siblings or fed up with annoying homework, I went off on a blue moon stroll. My place of refuge was our attic where I had used a dark blue woollen blanket to build a secret nest for myself. There I could snuggle up and imagine that I was on a blue moon stroll, even if it was just to avoid having to do the washing up. My blue moon stroll, a term which has stuck with me until today, meant that I wasn't available for anyone or anything. «Alice is on her blue moon stroll», everyone would say, and I was off the hook. Back then I consistently used blue ink, cheered for whichever sports team was wearing blue kit and even my craftwork always featured various shades of blue. I also thought that the phrase «feeling blue» had been coined just for me, particularly when history of art appeared on my timetable. Back then I often felt the temptation to abuse the phrase as an excuse to doze off during lessons, simply because I found the topics taught in the subject boring and monotonous. I can't be sure whether that was down to the particular teacher or my lifestyle at the time, but it happened on a regular basis. My interest in the subject was only aroused when we started learning about Picasso and his blue period. He had devoted four whole years to my blue! I was ecstatic, felt deeply honoured and my issues with feeling blue and dozing off came to an abrupt end.

The colour fixation of my childhood days stayed with me into adult life. Different colours for appointments, making them immediately clear and well-ordered but admittedly also making them look a bit like something from kindergarten. Red and yellow, purple and green dots spread out over each month, the red dots appearing more often than the others. My favourite, however, are the blue ones. Those are for appointments close to my heart. Today seems to be one of the lucky days, since I'm greeted with a shiny blue dot when I open my diary. «Send off tax return» it says, in bold capital letters. Irritated, I re-read the entry. Why on earth had I marked this entry with my favourite colour? Nothing about the task seems at all pleasurable to me and filling out the necessary forms definitely isn't one of my favourite pass-times. Still, I'd chosen blue and thus made taxes something personal.

I can't work up any enthusiasm and really don't feel like tackling this unpleasant task. In the olden days before iPhones I would have distracted myself from the task in hand by leafing through my tatty old diary, drawing stick-men. Or by trying to decipher words hidden beneath stars and squiggles I'd drawn there sometime in the past. I expect you remember diaries being these little books. Some of them beautifully bound in leather. Others with additional spaces for colourful post-it notes or business cards. Some even have a transparent pocket inside where you can insert a picture of your little darlings, your faithful cat or a beautiful romantic sunset. Or occasionally even just a picture of Brad Pitt. I have always marvelled at who and what I got to see in all these pictures when people opened their diaries at the end of a meeting. The dream car was no exception; many a wife had to make way for that. And all these little books were adorned with squiggles, scribbles and colourful notes, all of them, without fail. I was by no means alone in covering my diary with that sort of artwork. Apart from my random scribbles I was also in the habit of entering my dates and appointments in abbreviations and then I always imagined what would happen if I suddenly disappeared and really cool people had to try and work out what they all meant. A bit like in TV crime dramas where the detectives always manage to decipher even the most confusing entry within an impressively short time. They had my full admiration. I, for my part, was not blessed with such successes, since my own cryptic entries became seemingly nonsensical within a very short time and I found it impossible to make any sense of them at all. I vowed to improve my methods, switched from analogue to digital and started to note down my appointments in unambiguous words. However, my childlike colour schemes remained a permanent feature.

I am still staring at the blue dot which marks the reminder to send in my tax return. Blue, round, personal. That reminds me of a major blunder I committed with regards to blue. Years ago I lived and worked in the historic centre of Zurich. I had a charming apartment there in a period building, with generous rooms and a terrace outside the bathroom. It was beautiful! Since however it has been in a public building and I worked there as a public servant, people didn't seem to quite understand that I wanted to live a private life in my apartment. Perhaps I should have stuck a blue dot to my apartment door, but unfortunately that hadn't occurred to me at the time. In any case it was one of my duties to decorate this stately building and the surrounding square with flags on public holidays. Flags of Zurich that is, which are square and separated into triangles by a diagonal running from top left to bottom right. The top triangle is white, the bottom blue. For me, however, it was always clear that blue was the colour of the sky and therefore had to fly on top. Guided by my affection for all things blue I hoisted all the flags around the square upside down, which resulted in much ridicule, a serious crisis among the old residents and a headline in the evening papers.

Blue dot, tax return, I know. I can tell you as many stories as I like, the dot will still be there. My motivation is still limited, very limited indeed. I'd much rather wash the floor, water the plants, have a coffee and read the papers. And go shopping. Even to buy new ink cartridges, and for those I'll have to walk quite a long way. I get an unpleasant phone-call out of the way, make myself another coffee and sort the washing, even though I know that the laundry room is booked and I won't be able to actually do my washing. I turn up early to a meeting which against all expectations results in early consensus so that I find myself leaving again after only a short while. On my way home, I don't meet anyone I could stop for a chat with and now I'm back here, sitting in my now squeaky clean, freshly aired and meticulously tidy apartment. It almost feels a bit uncomfortable.

The dot is still gleaming, unchanged, in a beautiful blue. Why on earth had I awarded my favourite colour to this annoying task? It simply doesn't fit. Blue makes wishes come true, as I often say, and that you're blue ribbon. I've whispered that in your ear. And we both laughed. Miraculous blue, believe me, you said, blue promises wonders. Secretly, I even consulted a «Book of Answers» on the meaning of the colour blue in my life.

«It'll bring you luck», the book said.

Fabulous!

But why then... For goodness sake, that's enough. With a few clicks I change the entry to an everyday black, that's definitely much more appropriate. I regard my new choice of colour with satisfaction and have to laugh about my foolish behaviour. I sit up straight and put an end to silly procrastination.

Orange

With a quiet ringing sound the shop door closes behind me and I find myself standing in the middle of a wonderfully relaxed chaos. I take off my sunglasses and rummage around in my handbag, trying and failing to find my glasses case whilst watching the fascinating display of a tiny tot throwing himself to the floor in a noisy temper tantrum. Nobody apart from his already pretty stressed-out mother seems to be taking any notice of him. She tries to calm him down, but doesn't succeed until she lets him choose a Capt'n Sharky book. Peace returns to the children's bookshop, interrupted only by the occasional sound of quiet giggling. I love this place! The walls are lined with bookshelves from top to bottom, hundreds of books standing there in neat rows - inexhaustible colourful temptation.

I find the glasses case at last, put away my sunglasses and begin my search for a birthday present for Nico. As usual, I go straight for the new releases which can be found in waist-high boxes, sorted by genre. «Witches, Monsters, Ghosts» it says there in neat writing. Nico loves spooky stories. He enjoys being a little scared, but insists on a happy ending. I look through the picture books, linger here and there, leafing through a few pages or sometimes even the whole story. Amazing, the stuff I can find here! The world around me is all but forgotten, time literally melts away as I thumb through the books. Time must pass faster in bookshops, there can be no other explanation, I'm sure of it. I am lost in the arduous life of a blue monster that's miserable because a small boy doesn't allow it in his bed at night, when someone suddenly laughs out loud right next to me.

I nearly jump out of my skin with surprise, then look slightly to the right and there they are, the orange socks. There's somebody actually wearing orange socks! I look up and at that moment we each realize who the other is.

«Phil?»

«Alice!»

«Are you back?»

«I...Alice!»

We carry on like that for a while, we hug, we laugh and can't quite believe we've bumped into each other like that.

«Nice socks», I whisper and we both grin at each other. Our story had started orange. It's been a long time but it's obvious that neither of us has forgotten.

We had first met at the Zurich Riviera. That's what we called the place on the river Limmat between Quay Bridge and Water Church. Eight steps leading from Limmatquay down to the river. Perhaps they still carry this name today, but I'm not sure. I used to enjoy sitting there, devouring one book after another. I was in my third year of secondary school back then and it was my bright orange hair phase, which resulted in constant comparisons with Pippi Longstocking. I myself thought more along the lines of Vivienne Westwood, without having any actual interest in fashion. Back then, however, this Ms Westwood had declared that she was designing fashion for heroes and with that she immediately became my idol. And of course I adored her orange hair.

Anyhow, I was lounging about on the stone steps, lost in an imaginary universe, continually blinking in the warm sunshine and having to screw up my eyes to be able to read. It was really quite uncomfortable, this shimmering whiteness.

«How about a pair of sunglasses», said a dark voice to my right.
«Ha-ha, yeah right, sunglasses! I accidently dropped them into the Limmat yesterday», I replied brusquely and added «unfortunately» to sound a bit more polite. I couldn't stand being disturbed when I was reading. Before I managed to finish reading the next sentence,

however, a hand holding a pair of sunglasses appeared in my field of vision. They had an orange rim and blue lenses and were absolutely amazing.

«They go with your hair, I'm sure you'll look great in those. Go on, try them on!»

I jerked my head back and laughed out loud. A young man was crouching next to me, probably a few years older than me. He had untidy blond hair which was sticking out from under a straw hat. The ribbon around the hat was purple, his eyes a striking light blue and his shirt bright orange.

«A bit too much orange, don't you think?» I said – and that's how we met.

«Alice suits you really well», Phil remarked casually when I introduced myself and then muttered the name a few times to himself.

I fell in love with him immediately and before the day was over we were Phil and Alice, inseparable and only ever to be found together. We roamed the streets of our town and enjoyed each other body and soul. He wore his orange shirt day in, day out and it was only a matter of time before I followed suit and started skipping around in a batik dress in shades of orange. We really did skip around a lot and probably behaved rather childishly, but we didn't see it that way back then. We were so madly in love that we lost all sense of reality. His sunglasses became my trademark which I wore regardless of the weather. Inside or out, the sunglasses always sat on my freckled nose. Naturally, that led to quite a few arguments with my teachers which resulted in me having to do extra work as punishment on numerous occasions. I didn't mind that all though, and counted the hours until we would see each other again after school. He felt the same.

We take turns reminiscing, pause, smile, just look at each other. It feels really good to see him again. It feels completely natural which I find somewhat surprising after all this time. Everything is so simple with Phil, I'd forgotten about that.

«Will you have time for a coffee afterwards?»

«Sure, coffee, good idea. I'm looking for a book, though, for my goddaughter Hanna. She's ten. I'd like to find one she'd be able to read for herself, but that's also good for reading aloud. Any ideas?»

We rummage through the appropriate section, tilting our heads slightly to the left in a synchronised movement so that we can read the titles easier.

«Momo», we both exclaim at the same time, look at each other in surprise and start laughing.

«Just like old times! Good idea, and even better because the book is orange.»

He picks up the book and glances over the text on the back cover.

«Do you remember when we tried to stop time?»

How could I ever forget? Back then we were convinced that we could achieve absolutely anything, even stopping time. We were genuinely surprised to find that we were unable to pull it off. Like I said, we'd lost all sense of reality.

«And you, are you looking for anything in particular? Something for your children, perhaps? Do you even have children?»

«I'll tell you all about it later», I promise. «Should we go?»

We get «Momo» gift-wrapped and step outside onto the shadowy cobbled street. A mild spring day beckons. We stroll through the streets and after a short while we arrive down by the river, at a pleasant café on Hechtplatz. He gently strokes my hair, winks at me and whispers, «Grey instead of orange, it suits you. Now we're the same.» We both sit down and don't quite know how to tackle all the impending questions.

«I remember our music when I look at you. That record... you know... what was it called? It had a strange cover, a wild pattern of some sort... do you remember?»

«Do you mean Michael Franks?» I ask, somewhat surprised. Hesitantly, I hum the tune of «Antonio's Song», our favourite from that amazing album. It was a vinyl record with an orange cover, probably showing reflexions on water, but it was hard to tell. In the bottom right hand corner a butterfly was fluttering into the picture. We used to listen to those warm, sometimes melancholy songs at home and on our Walkmans and couldn't get enough of them. In the end I had to throw out the tape because it was all stuck together and wouldn't play anymore. The record, however, is still on my bookshelf at home.

«Yeah, that's right – our rainbow-song!»

Phil beams at me and starts humming along.

Finally, he leans back and looks at me expectantly. I tell him about my life after he left to study in Edinburgh, never to return. I tell him about my initial incapability to cope without him, how I spent whole days just staring into space as if he had died, how I annoyed the postman with my incessant questions about letters from you which came less and less frequently. I tell him about the time I cut my hair down to a few millimetres and started from scratch at last, fell in love, got pregnant immediately. I talk about my two wonderful children, about bringing them up on my own for years, good years. About my grandchildren. And about my sometimes turbulent life and my persistent luck in meeting all sorts of wonderful people. And my luck in general.

Now and again I pause in my account to just enjoy the moment and his undivided attention. We laugh a lot, sometimes heartily, sometimes quietly, even a little bashfully. I even confide in him that after his departure,

I started to meticulously collect all things orange so that I wouldn't forget my first love. Slightly embarrassed I describe the transparent plastic ring with a small flower hidden inside it, the cards, numbered from 0 to 107, with number 82 missing, and the tiny dog. I tell him about the pebbles from the sea, the bracelet made out of wooden beads. All of them orange. When I mention the batik dress which still hangs in my wardrobe, he takes my hand and we both sit there in silence for a moment before we both burst out laughing.

«How embarrassing!», I cry out.

He, however, shakes his head and confesses that in summer he still wears my necklace with tiny glass beads in orange and that his wife is always teasing him about it.

The coffee gets cold, we are nowhere near finished. Spellbound I listen to his account of his life in Scotland, the love he found there, his late fatherhood. I like the joy evident in every word he says about his family. There's quite a bit of pride too. He still speaks with his hands, hasn't lost the mischievous look in his eyes. We talk about our time together, which ended so abruptly. We wonder why and how we lost touch, exchange contact details and only pause when the sun disappears behind Uetliberg. It's markedly cooler now.

«Come, let's go for a walk», he says, and calls for the bill. I like the idea a lot. Time, I want more time with him, there's so much more to tell. He gives me a nudge and says:

«We simply need more time together.»

Without a word he drapes his jacket around my shoulders, takes my hand and we set off across the square in front of the Opera House towards the lake.

«At least there are people here!», he remarks joyfully and is thrilled like a small child when he looks at all the colourful chairs standing freely all over the square and finally spots a pink one among them.

The area around us gets quieter as we walk in the twilight and I feel like we only saw each other yesterday. We sit down in the beer garden at the tip of the Zurich Horn. The round table right at the edge is free and allows us an uninterrupted view of the lake. There are a few colourful lanterns hanging here and there in the giant sycamore trees above our heads, giving the place a fairytale-like atmosphere. We sit there, enjoying every minute together, chatting about the old days, about our hopes and plans. Soon the first street lights appear as orange dots in the bluish shadows along the banks of the lake.

«When are you flying back?», I ask at some point and realize immediately that that's completely irrelevant.

«In just a couple of days' time...»

He hesitates briefly before adding:

«It doesn't matter very much though, now that we

know where to find each other – and I won't disappear for quite so long this time, I promise.»

That's good, I'm happy with that. We carry on talking for a long time, sitting under the trees, listening to each other. When the lanterns go out we leisurely stroll back into town.

Red

It's seven o'clock in the morning. I'm standing in my kitchen holding a cup of coffee in both hands and staring blankly at the rainy day outside. It's really foggy too. I start at the sudden noise of a door banging somewhere in the house. I put the empty cup in the sink and try to collect my thoughts. I need to concentrate since it's moving day after tomorrow. So what's next? Rather helplessly I stare at the already packed boxes and realize that I have no idea how to manage it all.

The first five points on my list are already ticked off. After three attempts, I still can't decipher point six so I skip to the next line and see that points seven to ten all refer to the same task. Seven: Clear cellar. Eight: Definitely clear cellar. Nine: Now! Cellar! Clear it! Ten: CELLAR! There's no getting away from it. A miserable day indeed.

It's cold and gloomy there, but it's not as bad as I'd expected. While I wait for my eyes to adjust to the semi-darkness I let my gaze wander over stacks of my belongings until I spot my traffic signs. They're right at the back of the room, leaning against the wall underneath the barred window. Grinning broadly, I carry them out into the hall so that I can get a better look at them. I remember the night-time scenes when we took them all down. The fact that it was illegal to do that didn't bother us at the time, and we never got caught. Once it was a close call, I think that was when we were taking down the stop sign, but like I said, we were always lucky. I vaguely remember unscrewing the first one, the only blue one, «mandatory direction of traffic» its clumsy name. It all started with this sign.

Later, others followed, all of them in red and white, some with black as well. Red, white and black, a colour composition we are familiar with from earliest childhood: red as blood, white as snow and black as ebony - and although traffic signs are nothing whatsoever to do with fairytales, the colour combination inevitably reminds me of the beautiful princess. The topmost sign has always been my favourite. No entry, it tells me. It has survived well, if a little faded! The next one is the stop signal, the only one with eight corners. All the others are triangular, warning of various dangers. The one with the black exclamation sign in a white triangle is an absolute gem! The funniest one, however, isn't here anymore, I've given it away. It was the «No Motor Vehicles» sign, but we replaced the original picture of a black car in its middle with a VW-Beatle and that looked really cool! I'm definitely taking these with me, no question about that. But where's my favourite sign? «No Entry»? Surely it was...

I rummage through the shelves, look under the dismantled table and behind the clay pots which have all seen better days. The sign isn't there. A red umbrella which doesn't even belong to me. Eight cardboard tubes, boxes with old paperwork and all sorts of packaging. Plenty of bits and bobs, no «No Entry» sign. Where could it be? I sit down on the kitchen stool which has a leg missing, try to keep my balance and rack my brain trying to remember what on earth I might have done with my favourite sign. Then I remember Marcus. I'll have to ask Marcus. What a convenient excuse to put packing on hold for a while!

Three floors up and five minutes later an exceedingly friendly assistant answers my call and reassures me that Mr Geerfeld would call back as soon as possible... Yes of course. Marcus had always been the most industrious of our clique, the leader of the quintet. Somewhat disappointed I try to plan my next steps when suddenly he actually calls back.

«Marcus, so good to hear from you!»

«Listen, I was told it's urgent. What's happened? Are you ok? I haven't heard from you in such a long...»

I don't let him finish.

«Nothing major really», I reassure him. «I just need

to ask you something, albeit something a bit weird.»

After a short pause I continue somewhat uncertainly:

«Do you remember our collection of traffic signs? Do you know by any chance where my «No Entry» sign might be? I... well, I'm in the middle of packing because I'm moving, or rather putting my furniture in storage because I need to move out, but haven't found a new apartment yet... and well... I simply can't find that sign anywhere. Any ideas what we might have done with it back then?»

«You're kidding me, right?»

«No, no, I mean it, it was my favourite...»

«Have you gone completely mad? You've got nowhere to live and you're stressing about a silly sign?»

The line goes quiet for a few moments but then I suddenly hear him laugh quietly.

«You haven't changed much, have you? My goodness, Alice, it's been absolutely ages! I'd almost forgotten that time.»

We attempt to give each other quick summaries of our lives over the past few years, which of course turns out to be an impossible task. We keep trying though and soon discover that our lives couldn't be more different. Still, the intimacy of the old friendship is still there and I'm really happy to be speaking to Marcus again.

«Do you know what», he finally suggests, «we'll meet up tonight and get you another one of your favourite signs. What do you think, are you in?»

«Are you mad? You mean we go on a dismantling trip? Seriously?»

«Come on, don't be a spoilsport! Maybe we can even get Rachel to join us, and Frank too. I'll give him a call later; we still meet up every so often. What about Phil? Is he still in Scotland? That's where he disappeared back then, isn't it?»

I sigh quietly. Yes, I had completely supressed that part of our history. Marcus and Phil, who never quite got on, the repeated arguments between them, Marcus' total lack of understanding when Phil decided to study abroad and then broke off all contact. Old memories which suddenly come alive again.

«Oh Marcus. Yes, it was Scotland, and he's still living there. He's doing very well actually - I met him quite by chance a little while back.»

«Never mind, forget it.» He gives a short laugh. «Let's meet up this evening. My family is on holiday right now so that's ideal. Come on, go for it, it'll be fun, just like the old days!»

The thought of roaming the streets at night fills me with dread. It's all about my favourite sign though, isn't it? And so we agree to meet up later, I send Rachel a message with the details and quickly get back to my packing to take my mind off the forthcoming risky adventure.

Somewhat over-excited the four of us meet at the agreed place in the evening, equipped with all the necessary paraphernalia. Rachel is carrying her over-sized presentation folder, Frank has the tools, Marcus the gloves, and I will be allowed to choose which sign to take down. That's how it worked in the old days and seemingly nothing has changed, since the three friends end up looking at me expectantly once we've exchanged rather exuberant greetings.

«Where are we going?» asks Rachel, throwing her hair back nervously.

It's a grotesque situation. We are four middle-aged people, huddled together under two umbrellas, one red, one black, trying to shield ourselves from the drizzle. Our clothing is rather conspicuous, an old habit which has its origins in one of Frank's ideas. He always maintained that it's easiest to commit a crime when one is behaving conspicuously – at least if the crime is being committed in public. The focus should be on us and our appearance rather than on what we are about to do. Experience always proved us right and I am desperately hoping that it'll do so again tonight.

«We are utterly bonkers, do you realize that?», is my last, if rather half-hearted attempt to intervene and change the course of the evening.

«Aw, come on Alice, we're here now. Just once more, for old times' sake», is the answer I get – from Marcus of course, had to be. Off we go then.

Earlier in the afternoon Frank had given me a tip about which «No Entry» sign to take down. There's one in a side street near his studio. It's a good choice because it's still got the old varnish which means it's matt, not new and shiny. And on top of that it hasn't got a single bump, it really is a beauty. The first few screws come loose in no time. Obviously the way they're attached hasn't changed a bit in the last few years; Frank's equipment fits beautifully. Good for us. Within a few moments the sign is off and Rachel opens her folder.

«Dad?», chimes a surprised female voice from somewhere in the darkness and two young people gradually come closer. They are holding hands like star-crossed lovers.

«Dad, is that you? What are you... what are you all doing here?»

They stop and the tall young man holds his umbrella over his girlfriend's head, shielding her from the rain. Could that be Julia, I wonder while watching Frank's hopeless attempts to hide his tools in his coat pockets.

«Stella... hi Max!», he stammers. «What are you doing here? Weren't you going to the cinema?»

I had never been able to tell the two daughters apart. Despite their two year age gap they always looked like twins. So this must be the younger of the two, a very pleasant young woman. I wouldn't have recognised her if I'd met her out of context. Rachel looks at me inquiringly, but Marcus starts to laugh heartily and can't seem to be able to stop.

«You might remember Alice», Frank turns to his daughter, trying to explain the situation. «She used to visit us quite often. Do you remember? And this is Rachel, we've been friends for years, and Marcus...»

He stalls and now even I can't help laughing.

«You're stealing a traffic sign? Whatever next?»

The young man called Max doesn't say a word; he's obviously embarrassed by the situation. He whispers something in Stella's ear; she smiles at him and nods. With a quick «See you later» they say good-bye and swiftly disappear in the darkness.

By now Marcus has recovered and wipes his eyes with the back of his hand.

«Well that was fun! You'll have some explaining to do when you get home», he splutters, laughing again. Frank is just standing there, shaking his head slowly from side to side. He's a pitiful sight. Just when I want to apologise for the whole affair, he suddenly jerks his head back and shouts:

«This is completely absurd! You have no idea!»

He pauses for a moment and then carries on:

«He's a traffic manager! Max works for the city traffic department... that's simply... I can't believe it. He of all people!»

At that moment two bright headlights shine across our coats. Dazzled, I shield my eyes with my hand and can just about make out the orange and white paint-work.

«No, this can't be happening», I mumble and turn to the others, wondering what to do. This has taken us by surprise and so we do what we've always done in these kinds of situations. We all talk at each other all at the same time. The spotty pattern on my wellies lights up in the glare of the headlamps, Rachel's pink cape hides the large folder, Marcus pulls his yellow sou'wester lower over his forehead and Frank just stands there, dripping wet, holding his closed umbrella. We stick out like sore thumbs but the police don't seem to be taking any notice. The well-tried method of distraction from the old days proves useful once again and we get away scot-free, just like we always did. The police car carries on on its way, seemingly without giving us a second thought. It's almost a bit of an insult, we all agree, but the sense of relief is obvious on our faces.

Our chance meeting with Max and its possible consequences weigh on our minds for a bit, but then then Frank ends the discussion.

«Never mind. We'll see how he reacts. Let's just forget it for the moment.»

Chatting noisily we head for the little bar around the corner and don't leave until just before midnight. Arm in arm we walk to the car park, our spirits high. We only say our good-byes after I promise to hold a «No entry» exhibition as soon as I've found a new apartment. Everyone loves the idea and so I finally make my way home, clutching Rachel's folder.

Now that it's night the light in the cellar doesn't seem quite so gloomy and even the temperature feels more comfortable. I take another look at my new acquisition before carefully putting it with the others.

«It just had to be done», I quietly apologise to the «No Entry» sign with a shrug of my shoulders. «You really are particularly beautiful!»

Lost in thought, I look at the dripping umbrella in my hand, which doesn't even belong to me. It's red, my sister's colour. I promise to take it back soon, have a coffee with her. That sounds good. She's simply the best, I always say. I couldn't do without her, I think to myself and lock the cellar with numb fingers, listening to the gentle splashing in the down-pipe. Looks like the rain's getting heavier again.

Green

The air is still cool and the breeze feels pleasant on my naked legs. For the moment the only decision I have to make is what colour tablecloth to place on the round garden table. The original paintwork is covered in little dents which give the impression that the metal is painted with spots, but the surface still reflects the light brightly and unbearably whenever the sun hits it through the branches of the tree. A tablecloth is therefore an absolute must and its colour, as I said, my only challenge at present.

Today I decide on a pale yellow tablecloth with faded green and orange stripes running across it and matted tassels along its edge. With a sweeping move I spread it across the table before smoothing it with my hands. I love this ritual, the start of a new day. The deep blue glaze of my coffee cup is a nice contrast to the colour of the cloth. It's purely coincidental, but on this glorious morning, it's like the icing on the cake. Contented, I let myself sink into the weather-beaten wooden chair, put my feet up on the next one and stuff a boldly patterned cushion behind my back. I'm reminded of Africa, of proud women with long dresses in bright colours, of heat, sand and endless plains. Nothing in this garden is anything like that far-away continent though. Everything around here is so green!

I feel very contented sitting under the sprawling branches of the imposing ash tree, spreading over the garden like a roof. It doesn't belong to me, this magnificent garden. It belongs to my friend Lena. She's off travelling in foreign lands for six weeks and has asked me if I would look after her house for her. A very lucky coincidence, since I'm looking for an apartment, l unsuccessfully looking, but not finding one, and all my possessions are in storage. So this was very convenient.

«All you have to do is water the plants and collect the mail», she said, and that sounded marvellous. I soon noticed though that I didn't seem to be able to do this flowering glory justice. I got the impression that the plants were desperately missing their usual gardener.

«I'm doing my best, I promise you», I say out loud. I look around, somewhat ashamed.

«I'm talking to flowers now», I say to myself and have to laugh a little. Shaking my head, I get up, finish the last drop of coffee and make my way back into the house to water the indoor greenery. That takes quite a while because there's a lot of it. I do love this ritual as well though. I go straight for the green watering can since the metal one is much too heavy for me and it seems that I must have left the yellow one at the back by the roses yesterday. I put too much water into the can and consequently find myself unable to lift it. Laboriously I drag it out to the lawn, pour off some of the water and straighten up with a groan, massaging my lower back.

«You move worse than me!» I hear my neighbour's teasing voice. She is coming over at snail speed, pushing her Zimmer-frame.

«You can say that again!», I call back and take a few steps towards her.

«How's your foot today?»

She tells me that it's getting better and that she's getting increasingly fed up with her stupid waking aid. I admire her determination. She broke her left ankle two weeks ago, but despite that she still insists on completing her daily march up to the street and back, even at the ripe old age of eighty three.

«Just imagine, Frieda, I've started talking to myself lately. It's really quite embarrassing!»

«Ha, I know that sort of thing only too well!» She winks at me happily and hobbles off. I then sit down on the sun-drenched lawn, tie my canvas shoes properly and lie back for a moment in the soft warm grass. I take a deep breath, inhale the fresh scent. Just one more minute...

Eventually I pick up the watering can with an air of determination. Two floors up I start my watering circuit, filling flowerpot bases one after the other. I carry out this meditative task, quietly humming a little melody, when I suddenly hear a scratching noise coming from the ground floor.

«Hello, who's there?», I call happily, put down the watering can and hurry to the staircase. I can just about hear a few hurried footsteps on the floorboards before the front door slams and I'm alone again.

«Just you wait», I mutter to myself and arrive downstairs before I've had a chance to work out what I was actually going to do. I look around the house, searching every corner, but it's completely quiet, nobody in sight. I'm not sure what to think; had I imagined it all?

Slowly I make my way back upstairs and continue my tour, turning one or the other pot a little more towards the light, absent-mindedly stroking the odd delicate leaf.

«Don't panic, there's got to be an explanation», I try to reassure myself. It doesn't quite work though, and I'm left feeling nervous and unsettled. Once back downstairs, I look out into the garden and then go sit down on the green bench by the door. Relaxation is out of the question though. I keep looking around, unsure of what I'm actually hoping to see.

«I don't like this», I say out loud. «This isn't good.»

Here I go again, talking to myself. I just have time to think, «I can't go on like this», when I hear it again. Tentative steps, back there by the letter box. In a flash I'm on my feet and running around the side of the house, but all I get is a fleeting glimpse of a swishing ponytail under a yellow hat.

«What's going on?», I shout after the disappearing figure. «Just wait a moment! Wait!»

I don't stand a hope of catching up with the intruder since I don't know my way around the tangled undergrowth behind the house. Had it been a woman? What did she want and why did she run away when I appeared? I try to recall what I saw: black hair, bound loosely under a yellow hat. What colour were her clothes? I can't remember which immediately makes me feel really stupid. I turn back and as I walk past the letter box I look inside. There's a brown envelope in there, made from rough paper and covered with two rows of colourful stamps and numerous postmarks. Intrigued, I look at it more closely. It's got my name on it, forwarding address, all in order. I can't decipher the country of origin though and the postmarks are completely unknown to me.

«Definitely time for another coffee», I say to myself. I'm obviously failing in my attempt to just think rather than speak out loud. I stand in front of the espresso machine, impatiently waiting for the hissing noise which signals that I can fill my cup. I then sit down on the grass, turning the envelope back and forth in my hand, unsure what to do. Finally, I rip it open with one swift move and pull out a stack of paper, held together with a blue paper clip. I have to read the contents three times before I understand what it all means. A solicitor's office in San José in Costa Rica is asking for my immediate reply. They say it concerns an inheritance and that I'd receive further details once I've got in touch.

«What? But that's... it can't be!», I call out in surprise and this time I couldn't care less whether I'm talking aloud or not. The paperwork is drawn up in Spanish, English and German; it's even certified by a translation agency. Contemplating the situation, I put the papers aside and lean back. Just take a deep breath, wait for a bit, just one moment...

...Slowly I come back to my senses and for a brief moment I'm not sure where I am. I'm missing the familiar sounds of the city; all I can hear is the humming of bees and the distant barks of dogs. Somewhere someone is playing a tune on a guitar. I don't know it, that song. I gradually remember that I'm at Lena's, temporarily living in her house. Hesitantly, I squint up into the leafy green canopy above. The air smells of flowers, freshly cut grass and summer. Had I fallen asleep? At any rate, I'm lying in the grass under the ash tree. I stretch my arms, sit up gingerly and knock into a half empty cup of coffee next to me. I swear under my breath.

«Come on, really! Coffee stains on my favourite

dress?»

Still pretty confused, I look around. Right next to me there's the dark green watering can, brimfull of water. The door to the house is wide open, the cat is curled up on the wicker chair - everything's as peaceful as ever.

I get up, still feeling rather dazed and confused. Rinse out the dress, that's got to be the first step. What was the trick with coffee stains? Cold water and washing-up liquid... or something like that. Taking two steps at a time I get to the upstairs bathroom, hold the hem of my dress under the tap and realize that the plants up here haven't been watered yet.

«But I've just...»

One look into the bedroom and the rest of the upstairs confirms what I'd noticed in the bathroom: Everywhere just dry soil. Dumbfounded, I stand in the corridor while a small puddle collects at my feet. When the doorbell suddenly rings I hastily try to wring out my wet dress.

«Just a moment, I'm coming!», I call.

«You don't have to shout like that, the door is open», answers a deep voice.

I straighten out my dress and hurry downstairs.

«Oh, you're not a woman after all...», I burst out and immediately clasp my hand to my mouth as if I could take it back that way.

«Sorry, what did you say?»

«...and why did you run away before? You gave me

quite a fright!»

«I'm really sorry, but I have absolutely no idea what you're talking about. Last time I was here was at the start of the week, when I put some letters through the letter-box...»

«But you were... I called after you!»

The postman looks at me with concern.

«I don't understand... Are you feeling ok, is everything all right?»

He has dark hair tied back in a ponytail, is wearing a yellow baseball cap and is scrutinising me top to bottom.

«Your dress is dripping! Are you sure you're all right? Is Lena not at home?»

I realize that I must be an odd sight. I explain hastily that I'm house-sitting, that Lena is still travelling and that I'm perfectly fine, really.

«Have you got anything for Lena? Should I accept something on her behalf?», I add and look at him enquiringly.

He smiles back at me, visibly relieved. He extracts a brown envelope from his voluminous post-bag. It's covered with numerous post-marks across two rows of colourful postage stamps.

«I'm looking for a Ms Lenzlinger because I need her to sign for a letter from...»

«Costa Rica!», I interrupt. «I can't believe it! It's all right, you've found Ms Lenzinger, that's me.»

I take the rough envelope and sign on one of those electronic gadgets he holds out for me.

«You know, I was dreaming about this just now. I'll be getting an inheritance!»

Confusion and worry reappear on the postman's face, but before he can work out how to reply I beam at him and ask:

«Oh, I'm so sorry, forgive me! I'm Alice, the house-sitter. Have you got time for a cup of coffee?»

With a wink he holds out his hand.

«Andy, Andy Brändli, postman. That would be lovely – so what were you saying about dreams?»

Brown

I've never liked the colour brown. Perhaps it's because in my earliest memories of brown I associate the colour with the corduroy trousers I had to wear, passed down from my brother. I wasn't happy about that at all. I desperately wanted my own pair of trousers, blue ones. But no, they were brown and I found brown really quite boring. Just like my hair – that was brown too. Not a pretty auburn colour like chestnuts or hazel with a dash of orange. No, my hair was just an ordinary brown without any redeeming qualities and I found it annoying, almost more so than the trousers. My sister on the other hand had beautiful hair, almost black and always shiny. I however – well, what can I say.

In my beloved books which were all about cheeky headstrong girls with individual ideas the heroines never had brown hair. Their hair was always special in some way, for example red or pink or yellow. I loved that! In one of the stories a girl spy even sported blue hair and I immediately picked her as my favourite – blue hair, that would have been quite something.

I was, however, stuck with my own hair and the corduroy trousers, brown and boring. I often wondered why the colour brown existed in the first place. Who'd invented it? Could brown have been a mistake, and a big one at that? No matter who I asked, I never got a satisfactory answer. Brown simply seemed to be there in everyday life, and particularly pertinacious in mine.

During the time of my most stubborn repudiation of the colour brown my world was entirely free from television. Instead, back then, we used to listen to the radio together. Really! On many a cold winter's evening we would snuggle up in front of the fire, sip steaming hot chocolate and listen, spellbound, to radio plays on DRS1. I loved radio plays. They were great!

Detective stories by Francis Durgbridge were very popular and my favourite was about Paul Temple and the case of Alex, where someone was being trailed by a girl in brown. I can't quite remember all the circumstances and I even think that the girl didn't survive the dramatic events, but those nocturnal pursuits got under my skin and have stayed with me ever since. While listening to the plays we imagined the most gruesome scenes, explored fog-shrouded alleyways and cast furtive glances around the sitting room. Whenever the girl in brown was waiting for the object of her desire in dark, gloomy rooms, with the persistent ticking of the clock on the wall the only noise in the eerie silence, we sat there with bated breath, quiet as mice. We froze in dark alleys and wrapped ourselves in warm blankets when she walked through the cold autumn night. The ominous footsteps, their sound always accentuated with a slight echo, made us tremble with fear and huddle closer together. It was these sinister scenes that led to some reconciliation between me and the colour brown because here, for the first time, I saw something brown that I actually liked, even though the girl in brown only existed in my imagination.

Reconciliation or not, thanks to my discovery of henna my hair became first orange, then red and finally dark red. I never learnt to like brown that much after all. I had even painted my recorder gold because I couldn't stand it in brown. Despite my aversion to the colour brown I spent my first three weeks at the Art Academy capturing my first pair of shoes on paper in a shaded pencil drawing. We called it «Schümmerle». The shoes were scuffed at the toes and my absolute favourites. And yet they were brown. My constant attempts to banish brown from my life were, it seems, not entirely successful, evident from examples such as chocolate. I was particularly partial to the deep brown of dark chocolate. I couldn't resist it. I loved chocolate and consequently pardoned its colour. I also came to love beautifully soft leather boots, made from dark brown suede. My «I'll only ever run about in a white nightie, playing the flute»-phase became the «I'll only ever wear embroidered jeans with leather boots and co-lourful ribbons in my hair»-phase.

All the accessories of that time were almost inevita-bly brown and even furniture didn't escape that trend. The combination of brown, olive green and orange seemed ubiquitous. Orange was great, I wouldn't have minded more of that, but to me the mix of brown and olive green was simply ghastly. Yet before I knew what was happening, our house was carpeted in brown, our kitchen tiled in olive green and my aversion towards brown cemented forever. Even that, however, didn't stop me falling in love with a brown-haired boy. Like I said, I never quite managed to keep brown out of my life entirely. It was supposed to be an exception, though, the «falling in love with a brown-haired boy». Nonetheless, it was this boy who finally succeeded in making me feel slightly more sympathetic towards the hated colour.

Irrespective of that I still didn't quite like the colour.

Until yesterday. The day was somehow special and shook my «brown-free, if at all possible»-world a little.

It started really quite ordinary. Everything was as usual, apart from the sun, which shone unexpected-ly bright and hot from a sky which was cloudless for once. I left the apartment, dressed much too warm, and had to return to change into something more appropriate for the temperature. That led to my missing the bus and then finding myself stranded on the outskirts of town because I'd missed the connection which would have taken me onwards into the countryside. The situation was further aggravated by the fact that a pipe had burst near the bus station, flooding the entire area with muddy brown water. Everything came to a halt. And so I sat on a wall with my legs pulled up, gently rocking back and forth whilst waiting for over an hour and all the while staring at the brown sludge sluggishly flowing past below.

I arrive late, of course, very late in fact, something that's only happened very rarely recently. I actually like being on time, I feel more comfortable that way, but that's irrelevant at the moment, seeing that I am late on this occasion. There's an atmosphere of near reverence in the room, the seats which had been arranged in a circle are all taken and the entire audience is listening attentively to the speaker. I try to sneak unnoticed to the back of the room, but the creaking floorboards scupper this vain attempt. I grab a chair, hang my bag over the back and sit down, relieved that I finally made it. The speaker smiles at me briefly but doesn't stop in her explanations. Instead, she continues to outline how the evening is to proceed. She demands concentration and participation. I am familiar with the scenario and gradually relax. The alertness of the other participants is evident, their interest in everything that's going on is obvious to see. I don't really take much notice of the other people in the room and after just a few minutes I find that I can't remember any details. I don't know who's representing who, who's got which issue or who's here with whom. There's movement in the room, I often stand up, sit down again, follow the events around me and communicate with others. We are required to get to the bottom of difficult situations and to resolve them.

Despite my alertness I flinch when I suddenly find myself opposite a person who stands in front of me at a respectful distance. I keep my head bowed in order to concentrate. A few moments later I subject my counterpart to a thorough inspection, bottom to top. The first thing I notice are the spotlessly clean shoes, gleaming at me in a matt gentian blue. They've got to be brand new. The meticulously ironed trousers are followed by a loosely fitting jumper with a light coloured shirt underneath. All in brown. Brown!

I simply don't like brown, that's my first thought. Gosh, how superficial you are, is my second. At last I lift my head to see who's looking at me from above all that brown. And there it is, that look.

How quickly the world can change! How little time it takes to turn one's world upside down!

Someone says something I don't understand. It sounds like a question. Do I have to answer? Do I have to do anything? I want to react, but can't concentrate on anything but these eyes. They are inquisitive, somehow familiar and a warm mahogany brown. Strangely enough, I like brown eyes, it's always been like that. Perhaps it's due to the colour of my mother's eyes, or Lena's. That old friend of mine from the days of kindergarten has deep-brown eyes as well, eyes that get a slight greenish tinge when she's angry. Like I said, when it comes to eye colour I'm rather more tolerant, perhaps even immune to my aversion.

We are still looking at each other, my counterpart and I. The most bizarre images appear in front of my inner eye and for a moment I feel like a comic figure with little thought bubbles drawn over its head which are gradually getting bigger. The topmost bubble is crammed full of aaahs and ooohs, exclamation marks and question marks. At least that's how I feel; I can't change the flow of pictures and just stand there, lost for words. The connection holds, straightforward and precise.

The minutes pass and I wish I had somehow miraculously worked out how to stop time. Why do we learn so many useless things, but never anything that truly matters? What use are square roots, chemical experiments or dates of historic battles when all I really need to know is plain and simply how to stop time? An old familiar question that I've asked myself many times before, and once again I regret that Phil and I hadn't been more successful back then. My wish doesn't come true today either and the time just ticks away. It really is frustrating. Motionless and mesmerised we look into each other's eyes. Mine blue, his brown.

«Blue suits you», he says at once, gesturing towards my dress with an elegant hand movement and catching me off guard.

«I simply don't like brown», I reply without considering my words for one second. Startled, I clasp my hand to my mouth. His face gradually distorts and countless fine lines appear around his eyes before he finally starts to laugh.

«I'm wearing blue shoes», he replies, «doesn't that count?»

I like his reaction, I like it a lot. The people around us are soon forgotten as we start a lively conversation, starting with likes and dislikes, eventually arriving at dreams and visions. From blue to brown and onwards to other colourful topics. My aversion towards the colour brown crumbles away with every minute, my favoured colour scheme expands with every sentence. Not that brown suddenly counts as one of my favourite colours, but it's got something, hasn't it?

Yellow

It's the burning of winter in Zurich tonight. The doomed season in the shape of a huge snowman figure filled with wood shavings and firecrackers stands at the very top of an enormous bonfire. A small platform, serving as the giant's pedestal, offers him a wonderful view of the festively decorated town. Smoking his pipe one last time, he awaits his fate. At six o'clock in the evening the bells of the old town churches ring out, the fire is ignited underneath him and the destructive spectacle takes its course. The faster the poor creature's head explodes, the more beautiful the summer will be. That's what tradition says, and the weather of the coming months once again lies in the hands of this pipe smoking Böögg, the winter bogey.

This year, Nico wants to be allowed to stand near the fire so that he can watch the spectacle close up for once. He's been pestering me about it for ages, but I don't like the idea at all. Crowds are not my thing. If my escape route is blocked, I panic. For the little ones, however, it's a magnificent spectacle! The horses galloping around the huge fire, the booming brass band playing, all the flags and colours. And so I promise – this year we'll go there together.

And then I catch the flu. Spring flu they call it since there seems to be a type of flu for every season. Anyway, I lie in bed most of the time, have no energy whatsoever; my head seems to weigh a ton, I have a runny nose and I can't imagine anything worse than being submerged in a crowd of people. With a heavy heart, I therefore call Nico to explain the situation. His disappointment doesn't make it any easier for me and when he finally tells me to get well soon I feel really bad.

«I know I'm letting you down. I'm so sorry!»
The other end of the line goes quiet and I assume he's put the phone down. But then I hear his excited voice.
«I can go with Dad instead, he promised me!»
«That's great! Brilliant, give my best wishes to Florian and go and enjoy yourselves!»
«I'll tell you all about it later», Nico shouts down the line, then there's a crackle and he's gone. Relieved, I sink back into my pillows. Moments later, Florian sends me a text wishing me a speedy recovery and promising to send me pictures. I can just imagine his ironic smile. He's well aware that I'm not a big fan of that occasion.

I really ought to free the plants on the balcony from their winter coverings and tidy up the flat. I don't feel like it though, my head hurts too much, springtime approaching or not. I just lie there, letting my eyes wander around the living room until they come to rest on the art folders that are propped up against the wall behind the cupboard. Why do I have five of them? It takes quite some effort to get up, but then I stand there for a moment before sitting down, cross-legged, on the floor. Two of the folders are black and slightly shiny; the other three are made from rough grey cardboard. All of them are tied with black linen ribbons which seemed to have been knotted together for ages, since I can barely undo them. I manage to untie one at last and as the folder opens I'm immediately catapulted into the past. Back to my earliest school days, out in the countryside, in Mr Hugelshofer's class. He taught the first two years of primary school. Such a wonderful teacher, we all liked him a lot!

Like pieces of a puzzle the memories come together to form a clear picture and I'm there, standing in my classroom. Six cast-iron pillars reach up to the ceiling, there are tall windows along three sides of the room, the polished desks stand in orderly rows. As I close my eyes, I can almost smell the brown, well-trodden Lino flooring. I loved my time at primary school!

I leaf through my drawings and come across a self-portrait which smiles back at me. I don't recognise myself in the picture despite the fact that Mr Hugelshofer wrote «Excellent, well done» underneath it in his accurate cursive writing. My eyes are almond shaped and I look almost Chinese. My hair sticks out from my round head in all directions; the stripes on my jumper are uneven. All sorts of brightly coloured drawings pass through my hands, literally overflowing with zest for life. To my great surprise yellow is the dominant colour.

The houses are yellow, mostly anyway, the flowers are yellow, people's clothes are yellow, cars are yellow and so is the sun of course. The sun had to be yellow. That's how it was back then and still is now. If there's a sun, it's yellow, even though it really ought to be gold. In stories, it's always described as «the golden sun». We sing «Oh you golden sunshine» but still always paint it in yellow. And so did I. I knew that gold would have been better, but I didn't have gold in my collection of colour pencils. Moreover, gold was reserved for particular objects. Objects I didn't come across very often, like crowns for example. Crowns were made of gold; I knew that although I had never felt drawn to little princesses - pretty dresses and ribbons weren't really my thing. My world back then was almost devoid of crowns. I much preferred to explore dangerous jungles, ride across vast deserts and hide in dark valleys. If, however, I happened to meet a king or chief on one of my adventurous journeys, they did of course wear crowns. Crowned heads wore pure gold, without exception.

Sometimes, so my father told me, sometimes even the horn of a unicorn was made of gold, but I was never quite convinced by that. I couldn't really imagine that it was true and so all my unicorns remained white and I continued to use yellow for anything that should have been gold, simply because I didn't have a gold pen. Or a silver one. When the packs of colour pencils suddenly started to come with 40 colours instead of the usual 12 I suddenly found myself owning a gold pen and my drawings changed accordingly, as I could see quite clearly from my collection. My world order changed, gold trumped yellow.

After just a short while I feel exhausted. I collect the pictures together and try to stack them into a neat bundle when a small sheet of paper comes loose and falls onto the floor. It is badly damaged and I suspect that I had crumpled it up at some point before trying to smooth it out again later. It says «For Alice from Viola» in untidy capital letters. I pick it up, turn it over and see two girls holding hands and beaming at me from the crumpled page. One of them is wearing a yellow dress, has yellow plaits and an oversized red mouth. The other is wearing a brown pair of trousers, a blue jacket and has totally dishevelled hair. Viola - I had forgotten all about her. Her actual name was Violet and she joined our school in year two. We called her Viola. Maths was not one of her strengths and every time she gave a wrong answer we whispered:

«Viola la la has no ide-a –a –a», among ourselves.

The memories flood back instantly and I feel somewhat ashamed because I remember how funny I found this kind of teasing back then. Violet. The astonishing thing about Viola was, however, that she never held it against us. She laughed about herself or us, it was never quite clear who she was laughing about. And she had a yellow school bag with Violet written on its side in big letters. I never understood why her bag was yellow when her name was Violet. She then moved away again in year three and I had forgotten all about her until now.

Carefully, I smooth out the crumpled drawing and put it back into the folder. And then I also replace all the other drawings, one by one, yellow suns, yellow flowers, yellow butterflies. Strangely enough yellow ended up representing some of the rather more unpleasant things later in my life, such as those pungent flowers in our garden that engulfed me in a yellow cloud whenever I walked past them. Or the postman's yellow car which took me to school at such an early hour every morning that I could never quite warm to it. The Latin exam papers were also yellow. I didn't like the subject or the teacher or the tests. Not that I started to despise yellow because of that, not at all. It just wasn't one of my favourites. That's why it's now such a mystery to me that I used it so abundantly in all my childhood drawings.

I tie the art folder back up again, replace it in its place behind the cupboard and get up with a coughing fit. It had taken such a long time for the colour yellow to find its way back into my life!

The first thing I remember is a little garden gnome I found while clearing up the attic. He's a golden yellow from head to toe, smiling happily with his arms crossed behind his back. I couldn't resist him! A short while later the bathroom was stuffed full of rubber ducks of various sizes, all of them yellow of course. In my children's bedroom there were tall stacks of Disney paperbacks, printed on rough paper with yellow covers. When stacked in the correct order they formed pictures of Disney heroes on a yellow background. They were all there, even the Beagle Boys, Gyro Gearloose and Donald's three naughty nephews. And of course, one mustn't forget the «Duden», the rich canary-yellow edition of the German dictionary containing all the spelling rules. It's my companion and indispensable book of reference which is always given pride of place in my office.

When Uma Thurman declared war on the underworld in her skin tight, bright yellow outfit I became a major fan of everything yellow. Three years later «Little Miss Sunshine» flickered across the screens here and that was it for me. That yellow VW camper van! A life size picture of it hung in our entrance hall and tempted me on dreamy journeys on a daily basis. Ever since then yellow has been a welcome guest in my house and had been promoted above gold.

My head aches, I'm shivering, I'm desperate to lie down again. I collapse back onto the couch, prop my feet up on the armrest and watch she shadows on the opposite wall, cast by the cross grid of the window. Once again Viola enters my thoughts, Viola with the yellow school bag. Soon I doze off and in my sleep, I see you standing in the doorway on that Sunday morning. You hesitate on the doorstep for a moment, then lift up your head and stride into the room as if you were entering a ballroom. Every movement full of grace, as if you were gliding, and all in yellow. Your trousers, your jumper, your aura, everything a shiny yellow. You've put your hair up and your face is radiant as if you'd just won the top prize. I follow you with my eyes and it seems as if the room gets a bit lighter, happier and warmer with your every step. The walls drenched in a deep yellow, the floor flooded with light, the joy of anticipation almost palpable. You sit opposite me, smile at me and we start our work full of confidence. Like a coronation in yellow in springtime Berlin - that picture will never leave me.

I wake from my dreams with a start when the phone rings and seconds later I hear Nico's excited voice, telling me that Böögg's head had just exploded and that he'd seen absolutely everything and that the bangs had been really loud and there had been loads of people and horses... I smile to myself, look at the kitchen clock and know for sure that we'll have a beautiful summer this year - seven and a half minutes - it'll be great!

Purple

While the last few harmonies still linger in the concert hall, Etienne halts abruptly and despite his generous physique, he nimbly jumps down off the piano stool.

«Can you hear that? Can't you hear it?», he thunders.

«It all sounds too jubilant, too Schubert-like! This is Hilber! Brittle and strict, music from a world devoid of any embellishment!»

An awkward silence descends on the room, questioning looks are exchanged and here and there a restrained giggle can be heard. We lower our heads, our eyes fixed on the sheet music as if our lives depended on it. Still, I love the way our Maestro expresses himself. His unique colourful phrases often make us giggle even though they are usually full of criticism. Hilber? Who even was this Hilber? I turn over my music. J.B. Hilber it says, where the J apparently stands for Johann and the B for Babtist, as I find out from the text below, which doesn't really help me in any way.

«We are singing Hilber. Do you know who that was?»

Dressed all in black, he stands in front of us, his gaze commanding our full attention. It all appears rather theatrical when he continues in an emphatic voice:

«Hilber was for a long time the musical director at the Stiftskapelle in Luzern. This was a time when people were just beginning to dare to embark on slightly newer, more modern ways of composing church music. It was the time after the war, a pioneering spirit awakening all over Europe. It was also the time the first few concrete buildings were built.»

With a watchful eye, he scrutinizes every face in the room.

«Do you know how concrete sounds? What kind of tone it has?»

Now the befuddlement is complete, everyone's shaking their heads in total confusion and I can't suppress a giggle.

«They're angular and precise, the concrete buildings, almost austere. They represent the departure and the dissolution of ornate decoration. The music of that time should sound modern, yet not too much so. This feeling of being torn between tradition and vision is reflected in those harmonies. The desire to be innovative – yet not quite daring to.»

Our choir is a church choir. I'm in it, although I don't belong to any particular church and I'm not an active member of the church community. Martin simply asked me. I said yes, because it's great to see him once a week – and because I enjoy singing. It's a wonderful world that opens up when you sing. It inspires me no matter how passionate or dramatic the texts turn out to be. When we are then confronted with such bizarre questions by our conductor I know for certain that it was an excellent decision to take up singing again.

I love churches, the buildings I mean. I relish the silence and the generous scale of the open space reaching all the way to the top of the usually deserted rooms. They are places of power and strength which provide safety and peace, no matter how hectic life outside those walls might be. Wherever I am, there's always time for a church visit, be it the baroque and ornate or the bare and austere, tiny chapels or imposing cathedrals. They all share that stillness, a world of dreams within all that turmoil. Hallgrims Church in Reykjavik is one of my favourites. An imposing building whose tower reaches up into the sky like a spearhead. I immediately thought of it when I saw Minas Tirith on the cinema screen for the first time. The similarity with the white tower of Ecthelion at the back of the narrow plateau, which pushes up out of the rock like a wedge seemed unmistakable to me. Ever since then Minas Tirith and Reykjavik have been inextricably linked in my mind, if I can dare to voice such a heretical comparison.

What does concrete sound like? The question is still hanging in the room, Etienne's questioning look scanning our faces. We're just sitting there, speechless, none of us with even the slightest inkling of what concrete might sound like, what resonance a concrete room might possess.

I listen deep into myself, prick my ears, but hear absolutely nothing. I have no idea what concrete sounds like. I try to imagine the harmonies that float through churches as vibrations or as a fine, shimmering vapour. Most likely purple, I think. Reverent, awe inspiring purple. The colour of honour and dignity seems to harmonise well with virtual walls of concrete. Purple, which is also the colour of catholic vestments – in my imagination at least. Of course, that's highly simplified. I'm not familiar with the prescribed order of liturgical colours which is why in my imagination clergy always wear purple during religious festivities. In addition to the purple hues there are also some reddish tones, crimson I'd say. Also an awe-inspiring colour, that of dignitaries or Roman Emperors. Of course opinions are divided with regards to the correct colour terminology. I say purple, others say crimson - often it's unclear which colour people actually mean when they refer to one or the other. I have learnt that crimson is a mixture of red and blue in a proportion of four to one in favour of red, purple on the other hand consisting of a one to one mixture. Approximately. This was always just an attempt at a definition, but that's what I've memorised.

When I was a child crimson was entirely unknown to me, it didn't exist in my world. Purple however, did. In my children's books, there were magicians draped in purple cloaks and witches wearing pointy purple hats. I envied them all, would have loved to have the ability to turn our cat into a tiger or the annoying boy next door into a toad. For that I would even have dressed in purple. I also knew purple from the tabloids. There were piles of them lying about at my gran's house. The featured ladies looked positively royal in their evening gowns and I was in no doubt that they were actually cursed princesses - if the clock struck midnight they would all disappear and with them all the glittering purple dresses.

I'd drifted off in my thoughts and suddenly find myself back in our rehearsal room, somewhat bewildered. I still can't work out the sound of concrete. Our efforts to instil a modern, almost austere sound into Hilber's «Gloria» fail to produce the desired effect even the second time around. Schubert's Mass is still too engrained in us, its glory and jubilation, which incidentally seemed just as difficult to us and wasn't immediately successful. Back then the solution to the problem came from a surprising comparison. Etienne asked us to just listen for once, without thinking anything, to just listen. He gave us the keynotes of the Gloria and then playfully elicited a few chords from the black Bösendorfer piano. He looked up, smiling inwardly and asked:

«Do you know Autumn Leaves?»

Quietly the melancholy tune floated across the hall.

«Those are the same harmonies you find in the Schubert. Autumn Leaves. That's jazz. Sing the passage as jazz.»

He played it a few more times and then made us sing the Gloria again, with those sounds still lingering in our ears. To our astonishment Schubert became groovy and actually sounded a bit like jazz.

It's not always that easy for us to understand how exactly to interpret particular parts of a composition. Often we are so absorbed in reading the music that we forget about our diction or fail to listen to the other voices. The fallout is always immediate. We find ourselves faced with a wildly gesticulating Etienne, imitating our As and Es in an amusing spectacle.

«We don't sing a clear A. No, no! We sing an A, deep and open like an O, a hollow A. We sing as if we had hot potatoes in our mouths! Neither do we produce an E which sounds as if we were trying to out-do a siren. The E has to stay in the front of our mouth, we have to pout.»

The thing that really makes him lose his composure, however, are the Ss. The hissing, everlasting Ss. He really can't see the fun in those and jumps around in a triangle, a rather frightening sight to behold. Like I said, a Maestro with a powerful voice, screen-worthy in his performance.

We continue our efforts with Hilber's Mass and try to bring out its unembellished sound. While the soprano is practicing on her own, I'm back to thinking about concrete. I try to imagine concrete buildings and remember the huge chamber of a reservoir I visited during a guided tour. The arched ceiling was supported by angular concrete pillars and the lower part was painted in purplish blue hues. When the lights came on, sparkling reflections produced dancing waves on the walls. The water was gurgling quietly which lent the whole scene an astoundingly ceremonious note. Did concrete, therefore, sound like gurgling water? Like purplish blue gurgles? I don't think Mr Hilber would have been too happy about that. I think of motorway bridges, raised concrete structures spanning whole valleys, but even the soundscape of hissing rubber tyres doesn't quite seem appropriate for ecclesiastic singing. I remember my old school, also a concrete building. It's got a striking design and as it was a girls' school back then constantly engulfed in a soundscape of excited voices. Yet even this acoustic backdrop is unlikely to resemble the appropriate tone for Hilber. I'll never forget the wisteria plant which framed the entrance and whose blossom fitted that time so perfectly. We rehearsed rebellion back then, began to defy orders and joined the women's movement with great enthusiasm. Lilac was the colour of the day! The older students enjoyed wearing dungarees of that colour, us younger ones never quite learnt to like it that much. Instead, we made purple to our colour of protest, demonstrated for the freedom to do with our bodies whatever we considered to be right. We wanted to shock, to raise uncomfortable questions, to be heard. We wrote to the school administration, demanding that they use gender sensitive language and give preference to the female form, but since we wrote our demands on purple paper they were, unfortunately, barely visible.

«Alice, it's our turn!»

My colleague in the seat next to me gives me a poke and I lift my head, startled out of my reverie.

«Purple», I blurt out spontaneously, «concrete sounds purple with a hint of crimson.»

«Rubbish», comes the retort from behind me, «concrete sounds monotonous and dull.»

«No, powerful and robust...»

«...and velvety, with very little echo.»

And so it goes on all around the room, until Etienne resolutely asks for quiet.

«Great, you do know what concrete sounds like! Now sing Hilber just like that», he says as he sits down at the grand piano with a smile.

We practice once, twice, and more. Try to incorporate those newly discovered qualities into our singing. The unflustered, the powerful, the honest and the unfussy.

The angular, the simple and the velvety purple. The colour of the sound becomes more intense with every run-through, our voices blend together, fade away quietly at the end and the Maestro smiles to himself, finally contented.

Pink

Once again I'm stuck in a discussion about the colour pink. A discussion with Matilda. She is six years old and has her very own views on pink which she tries to make more palatable to me, as she has done many times before. I'm not really a fan of the sugary colours and so we debate, more or less seriously, the countless reasons for and against pink, whereby even the definition itself provides a contentious topic. If the colour contains just a smidgen of blue, we call it rose, is it too weak, we call it antique pink. It might contain too much white and therefore appear too sweet, or it's too deep and loses its radiance.

«Surely you love the pink clouds in the evening sky«, argues Matilda. «You're always raving about those.»

She scrutinises me, her head tilted sideways.

«Of course, they're beautiful! But they're clouds, they're allowed to be pink...»

She cuts me off.

«There you go», she calls out, obviously delighted. «So there's no reason we couldn't buy you a pink skirt. You're bound to look great in it!»

Even just the thought of wearing pink clothes makes me shudder, something Matilda simply doesn't understand.

«You know, there are some really nice pink animals too. You like those, you told me so yourself. Why then don't you want to dress in pink?»

I sincerely hope that the little girl isn't referring to pigs right now, something she denies in a fit of giggles when I ask her.

«No! Of course not! What are you like!», she blurts out and looks at me reproachfully.

«I'm talking about flamingos of course, they're beautiful!»

And there we go again, funny arguments flying back and forth because in my opinion flamingos are more orange than pink. She of course doesn't agree with that at all.

«Come on, let's go and check», I suggest. «There's a bookshop near here. What do you say?»

She's delighted with the idea and so we soon find ourselves in the subdued silence of the second floor, searching for an animal encyclopaedia. Apparently there are six different kinds of flamingo, it says, and according to the book they all look very similar. The colour supposedly comes from their main source of food, which is algae. By eating those their plumage turns various shades of pink, some more intense than others. If they didn't have access to the algae their feathers would fade and appear almost white. Luckily the pictures in the book are nice and colourful and show us that we were both more or less right. Reconciled, we leave the shop and saunter down to the lake. Our discussion about the difference between the various shades of pink is by no means over though. I almost know it off by heart. It's all about trying to find a rose coloured hairclip, a dress, a pair of tights or even a chair with one or the other invariably turning out to be pink instead. Which is a problem of course. And so once again the old debate flares up, the recurrent question of what pink actually looks like – or even rose.

It's time for some refreshment, that at least Matilda and I can agree on. Always. We sit in the shade of the trees near Bürkliplatz and play «Who gets ten first» while we wait for our drinks. It was originally invented as a bedtime game, but now we play it whenever we have to wait for something. It works thus: We pick a topic, animals, for example, or relatives, or places we've been to. Each of us then tries to come up with as many names as possible, saying them out loud and counting them off on the fingers of our hands until all the fingers are standing up. Whoever gets there first is the winner. So that's what we're playing today, and the topic is, unsurprisingly, pink.

«Pink, light red, flesh pink, rose, piggy-pink...», she rattles off at a speed I can't keep up with.

«Hmmm, hang on, light red - does that count?», I

try to intervene, but Matilda has already got to ten and smiles at me mischievously.

«I won! You're way too slow!»

We wander along the lake for a bit and I do my best to steer away from the topic of the pink dress. To my surprise, I actually manage to avoid the issue and we happily return home by tram.

«Can I watch TV?», asks a slightly grumpy voice from the sitting room. She's tired, snuggled up in grandpa's chair, looking at me expectantly when I check in on her.

«No, maybe later for a little bit... perhaps you could draw something or read a book...»

It's no good; she doesn't like either of my ideas. I have to think of something quickly.

«How about collecting all the pink things in the apartment? Who knows, you might find your favourite colour here somewhere.»

Matilda jumps up before I even finish speaking. I return to the kitchen and she runs around the apartment. Her task isn't easy since there aren't many pink things around here. There's the pink candlestick, decorated with little cherry red roses and dark green leaves, all in delicate ceramic. Also in pink, albeit pink with a hint of plum, a book by Luisa Francia. It's dedicated to 366 goddesses, a goddess for every day. My birthday is represented by the Pleiades who stand for the combined power of women, sisterly love and solidarity. I felt really honoured when I read it for the first time. Then there's of course rose quartz which brings me calm and serenity and keeps away annoying spirits. Truly essential. Also pink, although almost coral, is Paul, who's standing on my bookshelf, usually on top of a collection of fairytales in a deep blue. Paul is a sow made of plastic. I'm allowed to call him that because he insists that he prefers to be called a sow rather than a pig. I haven't a clue why he feels like that, but as far as he was concerned, there was no room for discussion and so I left it at that. He comes from somewhere far away, but didn't want to tell me where from exactly. He loves to be surrounded by mystery. His full name is unbelievably hard to pronounce. That's why I called him Paul. He likes it. He's wearing black shoes, blue trousers and a white shirt that's much too big for him. He loves to stick his hands in his pockets and watch me while I write. He is particularly chatty in the mornings because he spends the whole night thinking about things, or at least that's what he claims. He says things like:

«Stop thinking. Just write what comes to mind, you can ignore the rest.»

Other than that he spends most of the day reading or lounging about in the apartment. When we first started living together, I found it hard to accept the plastic scoundrel who was chatting to me incessantly in the mornings and giving me unwanted advice all through the afternoons. By now we're getting on well though, Paul and I. Matilda has met him of course and is totally crazy about him. She even takes him to bed with her every time she comes to stay overnight and of course he's the first thing she grabs on her quest for pink objects. The two of them are chatting in whispers and must be having a whale of a time, since I'm left to cook in peace.

«Three! We've found three. Have you got any more?»

She comes whizzing around the corner and falls flat on her face. Yet instead of cries of pain I hear a triumphant yell. She nimbly crawls under the couch and swiftly retrieves a small pink rubber ball.

«Four!», she cries.

«I don't even know that one, it must be Nico's. I seem to own more pink things than I realised! By the way, dinner's ready, you better go and wash your hands.»

I drain off the boiling water, place the grated cheese on the table and put an end to all things pink for the time being.

Only temporarily though, as I find out later. As soon as her teeth are brushed, her hair is combed and the little girl is tucked up in bed, covers pulled up to her nose, the topic of the day returns.

«I'm sure I haven't found all the pink things yet. May I carry on searching?»

This is our secret habit, lying in bed and talking until she falls asleep. That can take quite a while though! It is these moments, however, that I particularly love. These murmured conversations in the twilight.

«Tomorrow, and perhaps Paul can help you again.»

«You know», chimes the little voice from under the covers, «Paul told me a funny story today. He said he used to live in a house where all the walls were painted pink and that he liked it there very much. Really! Perhaps you should paint this apartment pink too, then he'll like it here even better! Can you imagine that?»

«No way, I certainly can't imagine that!», is my first thought, but she's already moved on to the next question. Would I tell her a story please, but not one from a book, no, it should be one of my own. Something that happened to me. And of course it ought to be a pink story.

«Now then... hang on...», I mumble, stroking her head. «I have to think of something... right: Do you remember how I went travelling last year?»

I hear a muffled «mm-hm», she snuggles up closer and gives me a nudge.

«I travelled north to a beautiful city. It's called Stockholm and I like the place a lot because the city is like something out of a fairy-tale, with palaces and gilded roofs. It's by the sea and you know how much I like that.»

I wink at her and she smiles at me sleepily before asking when we'd be able to go to the seaside together.

«When you're a little older, we'll go then, I promise! Well then... I explored this city on foot and by boat. Many of the sights can be seen best from a boat. It was nice and warm and the city was absolutely magnificent.

On the last day, shortly before I had to go back to the airport, I got completely lost, had no idea where I was and then I suddenly found myself standing under a sea of pink cherry blossom. I had just turned a corner and there I was amongst all this pink. It was stunning! I had never seen so much pink all in one place. In front of me was a wide space with a basin of water sunk in its middle. It wasn't deep, you couldn't swim in it, but it looked simply beautiful. The rest of the space was planted with hundreds of cherry trees, all in full bloom.»

Matilda looks at me in surprise.

«But that's loads! Was it a forest?»

«Hundreds was perhaps a little exaggerated, you know. I have no idea how many there really were. It was a lot though – and they were all flowering pink! There were a lot of people there, all of them bathed in a soft, pale pink light. They moved very slowly, as if on stage or in slow motion. Nobody spoke loudly, they were all just whispering. The branches were hanging low, the air was filled with a sweet scent. The sea of blossom floated like a delicate cloud above our heads. And all the people were taking pictures, just imagine that! The constant clicking of the cameras was actually rather annoying in that sombre atmosphere.»

«Did you take pictures too? Can I see them?»

«Yes, I tried, but unfortunately they didn't quite come out right...»

«And were the flowers really pink? Not rose-coloured?», she interrupted. «Are you quite sure?»

Now I do have to fetch the pictures, otherwise it'll be impossible to get her to sleep. No sooner said than done, I sit on the edge of the bed with the photo album open on my knees.

«What do you think? Are they rose-coloured or pink?»

Matilda sits up, casts a quick look over the pictures, rolls her eyes dramatically and then provides an absolutely clear explanation for when the flowers ought to be regarded as pink or rather rose-coloured. And I still can't tell them apart. Not at all. My problem. I have long given up trying to follow the Matilda-logic. I've got her right here after all, so she can explain it to me again and again.

Black

«May I join you?»

«Pardon?»

«May I join you?»

«But of course. Sorry, I was lost in thought.»

Slowly the man turns around and with a deep sigh, he sits down heavily next to me on the bench. The hand holding his walking stick is trembling slightly.

«Can I...»

«No, no, I'm fine.» He gives me a kind smile.

«The young! Always thinking you're obliged to help the likes of us!»

«Young! I wish...»

Oh dear, I'm sure he's after someone to talk to. I don't feel like talking.

And so we sit there, the two of us. The cobbles under our feet are shimmering in the heat. There's a dull silence over the square. The weather-beaten bench, which stretches around the mighty lime tree in a closed circle is painted a dark grey. It is not very comfortable and it's pressing painfully into my back in several places. When the church door opens at the top of the wide staircase to our right, we both turn our heads. A young woman hastily steps out into the sunshine. She sets a watering can down on the ground next to her, wipes her hands on her apron and reaches hurriedly for her mobile. The conversation is short and we can't hear it properly. She then snatches the watering can, obviously irritated, and runs down the steps, taking them two at a time. For a brief moment the sounds of the organ can be heard, before they are swallowed up again by the church when the heavy door slams shut.

«Are you nervous?»

Here we go. I shake my head ever so slightly. I really don't feel like talking.

«I'm only asking... because you keep turning your hat round and round.»

Irritated, I look down at my hands and keep them still.

«No, really, I'm not...»

«I like your hat. A proper hat, like it should be.»

I lift my head and look at my neighbour properly for the first time. He looks relaxed, sitting there in a white shirt, grey waistcoat and matching jacket. His tie is done up tight. That's got to be uncomfortable in this heat.

«It belonged to my grandfather», I finally reply after some hesitation. I lift the hat up a little and look at it pensively.

«Do you miss him, your grandfather?»

«No, no, I barely even knew him. He died when I was just three years old.»

I flip and turn the black hat, consider it from all sides as if I was seeing it for the first time, although I already know every seam, every tiny speck of dust on its felt. It's a Borsalino from Alessandria. That's what's printed on the ivory-coloured lining, along with the town's coat of arms. The sweatband is made from fine goatskin and embossed with the gold Borsalino lettering. The trim is slightly shiny and ribbed, the hatband wide and black with a bow. A true masterpiece despite its age.

«I just like it, this hat. It's a bit tight for me though. My grandfather's head must have been quite small.»

«I used to wear hats a lot. In the past. That was the proper way to dress for a man.»

A door slams behind us and someone calls:

«Hey, Oscar, everything all right?»

The man in the grey suit doesn't even turn around. He just lifts his hand and waves briefly. It's an elegant sort of wave.

«Yes, yes, everything's fine. And you? Hot today, isn't it?»

A «Phew, you can say that again!» is the answer, then the footsteps disappear again. All the while I'm staring blankly into space, turning the hat back and forth and trying to bring some order into the flood of thoughts in my head. My efforts are interrupted by the chatter of a class of schoolchildren, storming into the square from a side street. The teacher catches up to them in a few long strides and instructs the jolly crowd to be quiet, which doesn't however take effect until repeated several times. Her explanations about the historical building behind them are short and concise and then the colourful gaggle moves on, the sound of their chatter diminishing as they disappear between the rows of houses. Tranquillity returns to the church square. The heat is getting to me and I ask myself once again just how uncomfortable it must be with such a tightly bound tie.

«It's a Borsalino, isn't it?», I suddenly hear the old man ask.

Somewhat bewildered, I look up, pull myself together, put the hat aside and turn towards my neighbour at last.

«Wow, I'm impressed! How did you guess?»

«I recognise an original when I see one», he replies and winks at me happily.

«Memories are something quite remarkable», he adds somewhat out of context. He eyes me inquisitively.

«Are you all right?», he asks.

«Yes, I think so», I say and immediately realize how clumsy this answer sounds.

«No, that's not right, to be honest. I'm confused. There are so many things going through my head. I'm waiting and don't really know what I'm actually waiting for.»

«Waiting is a good thing», he answers without hesitating. «Waiting allows us to focus on things we would otherwise overlook. Waiting clears our thoughts, paves the way for the moment when the waiting has to stop.»

«Those are clear statements for once! Let me tell you, I love clear statements. And yes, I agree. I would however like that moment to be here already. I'm not very good at waiting. Still not.»

«That'll come...»

The rest of the sentence is drowned out by the howling engine of a delivery van squeezing through the narrow street to our left. A man jumps out of the cab and slides the side door open in one swift movement. We both sit there, watching him as he pushes his cap back a little, pulls a wreath out of the van, carries it up the stairs to the church and disappears inside for a little while before reappearing a few moments later and arriving back at the bottom of the stairs, having taken them at a run. He repeats the process three times, then gives us a brief nod, jumps back behind the wheel and speeds off.

«Always on the ball, the young ones», comments the old man and we both fall silent again. It's a peaceful silence.

«What were you trying to say earlier? I couldn't quite hear.»

He just shakes his head and nods.

«Tell me, what was it about waiting?»

«I think I'm waiting to be able to cope with loss», I reflect and startle a little at the realization that I'd said it out loud.

«Loss, yes, that's a heavy burden. It has a tight grip on you, won't let go, and every time you think it's becoming bearable, it hits you again like a bolt of lightning.»

I like him, this old man. He pulls my thoughts from my mind and puts them into words. I'd like some more of that.

«You know, I can't help you with that», he continues. «But if you feel loss, you must also have felt love. And that's a gift.»

I wait for him to carry on, but he just rests his sinuous arms on the bench and looks at me.

Suddenly there's the sound of birds twittering excitedly above our heads, then they fall silent as quickly as they started. By and by people dressed in dark clothes appear from all directions. There isn't much talking, most walk with their heads bowed, some carrying white roses. They climb the steps to the church, pause for a moment and then nod their thanks to the verger who holds the door open for each of them. The church clock strikes a quarter past two and immediately afterwards the church bells start ringing. Sombrely they resound through the town.

«I like funeral bells. Their sound is comforting in a way.»

«Yes, and warm too», I add. «Good for the dead and good for those left behind. Pacifying perhaps.»

He sits there quietly, his eyes closed, and for a moment I wonder if he's gone to sleep.

«Is that why you're here?», he suddenly asks. «A farewell?»

I only have time to answer with a short «Yes» before we're interrupted by a woman's voice.

«Oscar! There you are! I've been looking for you everywhere!»

There's the clicking sound of hurriedly approaching women's heels and a middle-aged lady appears in front of us. Her face is flushed, she's completely out of sorts and looks at both of us reproachfully.

«Have you been chatting to strange ladies again? Oscar, you can't do that. We've talked about this. And to run away like that. No. Not again.»

There's a brief pause.

«Come on, get up now, it's time go back.»

I don't like her bossy tone. She completely ignores my «It's all right, we've been having a lovely conversation», grabs Oscar by his left arm and tries to pull him off the bench. He resists, shakes her hands off and turns towards me with surprising agility.

«You've really brightened up my day, my dear. It's been a pleasure.»

He gives me a charming smile, winks at me one more time and gets up stiffly.

«You'll be fine», he mutters while trying to straighten up. «Just give yourself a bit of time. You'll be fine, you'll see!»

I jump up, help him to steady himself and plant a spontaneous kiss on his cheek.

«Thank you, thank you...You are wonderful!»

Before I can add anything else the woman urges him on to move. Could she be his daughter? Or a carer? I don't like her.

«Until next time!», I call after him and he waves back at me briefly.

I'm standing under the lime tree, feeling a little lost. I turn around, carefully pick up the hat, stroke the rim briefly and finally turn towards the church. When I stop to catch my breath at the top of the stairs, I see that Marcus is standing by the entrance. It's as if a huge weight suddenly fell off my shoulders.

«Hey, are you ok?»

«Yes. I thought I wouldn't make it, but then I had this wonderful encounter down there. With Oscar. Now I'm ready.»

«Oscar?»

«A proper gentleman. I'll tell you all about it later. Have you come on your own?»

«No, the others are already inside. I was waiting for you because I thought you might not want to go in alone...»

«Thank you. You're marvellous, do you know that?»

He smiles and puts his hand on my shoulder in a fine gesture.

«Come, let's go.»

White

The sand feels cool under my feet. I walk along the beach, my trousers rolled up and my jumper slung across my shoulders. With my trainers in my hand, I try to walk along the border between land and water, which must look like a funny little dance from the distance. Whenever I underestimate how far a wave will lap up onto the beach I get to feel the icy water. There's no way I wouldn't go barefoot though. The sea on my right looks dark with just the occasional white tip flashing up here and there. Its surface reminds me of the dark slate floor in the tiny house beyond the dunes that I left a good hour ago.

The widely spaced out beach bars that appear out of the darkness as I walk along are all boarded up for the winter and seem almost ghostly. The white border between land and water shows me the way, on and on, accompanied by the gentle murmur of the sea. The peace feels good after the turbulent times. Peter's unexpected death as well as the voluntary nature of his decision was very hard for me to deal with and I almost couldn't bear all the well-meant sympathy. Time for myself, that's what I wanted. That's why I left for the north, for the wide beaches which are almost entirely deserted at this time of year.

The choice of the little house was a gut decision. I liked the picture on the net and two days later I was on my way.

«It gets cold in here», my landlady explained repeatedly. «You have to put the heating on full.»

She had initially viewed me with a mixture of scepticism and concern. She was happy about the unexpected rental at the beginning of November, she stressed that several times, but she was decidedly uneasy about letting a woman stay on the beach on her own during this cold time of year. We get on well though, old Kate and I, and she waves at me every time I walk past her shop, wrapped up warm against the cold.

Today the sun once again managed to fight its way through the thick clouds. The afternoon felt almost spring-like which enticed me to make myself comfortable on the veranda. With a cup of coffee on the table and pen and paper at the ready I was all set to write. At least that's how I'd imagined the ideal circumstances, idyllic and focused. My thoughts, however, seemed to get stuck somewhere between my head and my hands and I didn't manage to write a single sentence. With total writer's block I sat there in the wicker chair until dusk. Slowly a damp, cold started to creep under my clothes but the sheet of paper in front of me remained untouched.

A gust of wind whips up my hair. I sit down on the sand, pull a shoelace out of one of my trainers and use it to tie my hair into a ponytail. Shivering, I put on my jumper and look around for a familiar landmark. Where actually am I? I recognise very little, nothing seems familiar at all. Far ahead I can see a bright shimmer above the cliffs, almost orange. It's hard to judge the distance, but I set off towards the light at a determined pace. Getting clarity, untying the knot in my mind, that's my aim. And so I go on and on, along the white line, continuing my dance with the waves.

«Hi!»
Startled, I turn around quickly.
«Did I make you jump? Sorry!»
Too late for an apology, I think to myself and come up with a half-hearted «Yes, you did rather.»
«The dancer of the night», a dark voice says, a voice whose owner I can barely make out to begin with. It's got to be a man, I can only just see his outline though. Slowly he comes closer, holding both hands defensively in front of his body and looks me straight in the face.
«It's all right. I thought you'd heard me. Don't worry, I'll be off again.»

He nods, adds a quick «Hope you get home ok» and disappears silently into the night.

«Wait!», I call after him. «Wait! Can you tell me where I am? I've completely lost my bearings. I have no idea how far I've come.»

Panting, I catch up with him at last.

«And do you know what that light is up ahead? It looks like the reflection of a fire. Could something be burning?»

«Are you a tourist? At this time of year? Where did you set off from?»

Once again I'm being eyed with a great deal of scepticism. Before I manage to say another word, though he explains that in the bay up ahead his friends are celebrating the birth of their first child.

«It's an old tradition here in our village.»

He pauses for a moment before adding:

«Why don't you come along? It's an impressive spectacle, believe me, you'll like it. I'm Ole by the way.»

«Alice. Are you sure you don't mind?»

With a wave of his hand, he brushes aside my concerns.

We walk quickly, it's got really quite cold. He tells me about his life on the island, about how he went away for a long time to get away from the close bond between the people here. He also tells me about how the frantic life in faraway countries didn't appeal to him either and how he finally ended up back here a short while ago. He speaks with great intensity, almost glowing with passion. I find him fascinating. I can talk to him with great ease, without being aware that he's having this effect on me. I paint a picture of my day to day life in town, touch briefly on my work, my concerns about the future. The words come flooding out, I take him with me into my stressful life, talk about my family, about how my life keeps changing course, about my dreams. For the first time I also manage to speak honestly about the loss of Peter. The final farewell, which I hadn't seen coming and which derailed me completely. Here, on this dark, autumnal beach, the words come naturally. It feels really good. When I finally tell him about my afternoon and the stubbornly blank piece of paper, he laughs out loud.

«Well you'll definitely have to write at least one word today», he says, grinning at me. «There'll be no getting around that.»

I don't understand his remark so I look at him enquiringly but he just waves my question aside.

«You'll see soon enough.»

When we reach the headland our view opens out over a bay, sheltered from the wind. A huge fire casts dancing shadows over the cliff beyond. There's something quite dramatic about the scene and reminds me of a film set. Ole has already reached his friends who are standing around the fire in small groups. He eagerly waves at me to come closer.

«This is Alice», he shouts loudly into the crowd. «She'll be our guest today, I've found her on the beach...»

He's briefly interrupted by scattered laughter, but then he continues:

«...she lives in old Kate's little House...»

Roaring laughter drowns out the rest of his little speech. Some pat my back sympathetically; others just look at me in astonishment and ask if I had enough woolly blankets. A young woman, who briefly introduces herself with «Pina, I'm the mum» presses a tin cup in my hand.

«Watch out, hot», she adds, «and don't take any notice of them! I'm sure you'll manage to warm the little house up eventually. I'm glad you're here - come, we're just about to start.»

There's the top of a hand knitted woolly hat just peeking out of her colourfully striped baby-sling. That's all that's visible of the tiny main attraction of the evening. Two boys whizz past me, Ole shouts something after them, but they just carry on running. Then he hands me a piece of paper and a pencil.

«Your turn, this is your personal challenge for today», he teases me. «Write your wish for little Isa on this piece of paper. Then you shout it out loud and throw the paper into the fire. The wishes burn, fly up and will be fulfilled. That's our tradition. Don't think, just write!»

I look around uncertainly, wondering who might be Ole's partner. I sit down on the sand, cross-legged. I pull the shoelace out of my hair, put it back where it belongs and slip my trainers on. A wish? My pencil hovers above the sheet of paper. The word comes to me in a flash and I write it down, somewhat clumsily, my fingers a little numb from the cold. Then I quickly re-join the others who have formed a wide circle around the fire. Nothing can be heard apart from the crackling and spitting of the branches breaking up in the fire. Pina and her partner clasp each other's hands and shout 'Health and Love' together. She crumples up her piece of paper and throws it into the fire, and he follows suit. And so it goes on round the circle. The children's wishes bring occasional outbursts of laughter since they include just about everything from «Wings» to «Magic powers». Ole is standing near a petite woman with her hair wrapped in a bright yellow scarf. I like the look of them together and once they've cast their wishes into the fire they slowly come towards me. They wait until I've shouted «Freedom» into the night, then the woman holds out her hand to me with a friendly smile.

«Lilja. It's nice that Ole brought you along.»

They make it easy for me. The conversation flows effortlessly back and forth, the grog helps it along as well and warms us to the bone besides. I shake many hands all round and try to remember all the names which is quite a tall order. We walk back to the village together around midnight and I say good-bye to my two new friends, having promised to come round for dinner.

It's freezing cold in my house. I remember the surprised looks and begin to understand the reason behind them. I pile wood chips onto the fire, put thick logs on top and watch the flames eating their way through the dry wood, hissing and spitting. Wrapped up in one of the knitted woollen blankets I sit by the fire for a long time, occasionally casting a look at the blank white pages carelessly strewn all over the kitchen table.

I get woken up by the cold and my entire body aches. Groaning, I scramble out of the armchair and wrap my temporary cloak tighter around me. Absolutely indispensable, these warm blankets! The dunes in front of the house are shrouded in fog and I can see my breath in the air as I step outside the door. The morning air is icy cold. With a shudder, I turn around and decide to go back inside to stoke the fire and make coffee. Out of the corner of my eye I just catch a glimpse of a stack of paper on the garden table, weighed down with a little crocodile. Graceful and all in white it sits there, looking at me expectantly.

«What are you hiding under your tummy», I ask curiously and carefully pull out a piece of paper.

«This is Alvar» it says there in broad handwriting. «He loves to be fed with words... and he's always very hungry, you can take our word for it! So just write and everything will be fine. Have fun and don't forget we're having dinner together the day after tomorrow. We're looking forward to it, best wishes, Lilja & Ole.»

I take a closer look at my new companion and run my finger across his scaly back. My crocodile is made from fine porcelain and absolutely delightful.

«Alvar, right?», I whisper. Taking care that he doesn't slip off, I pick him up with the stack of paper.

«Come Alvar, let's go and make sure you get plenty of food.»

Ursula Hess

I was born in Zurich in 1960, and I am still living there. My working life began as an administrator of a manufacturing company. It was during those years that I discovered my organizational skills and my talent for structuring processes. I subsequently reorganised various companies, wrote my first strategy papers and finally took on to large projects. But one day my life took another turn....

During the often turbulent times that followed, my love for writing always rescued me. It allowed me to turn thoughts into sentences. Writing them down on paper enabled me to forge bridges and to create my own world, which is my biggest passion. Besides that, I love people with dedication, bright eyes, blooming trees and the laughter from the heart.